Blastoff! Readers are carefully developed by literacy experts to build reading stamina and move students toward fluency by combining standards-based content with developmentally appropriate text.

Level 1 provides the most support through repetition of high-frequency words, light text, predictable sentence patterns, and strong visual support.

Level 2 offers early readers a bit more challenge through varied sentences, increased text load, and text-supportive special features.

Level 3 advances early-fluent readers toward fluency through increased text load, less reliance on photos, advancing concepts, longer sentences, and more complex special features.

★ **Blastoff! Universe**

Reading Level: Grade K → Grades 1–3 → Grade 4

This edition first published in 2023 by Bellwether Media, Inc.

No part of this publication may be reproduced in whole or in part without written permission of the publisher. For information regarding permission, write to Bellwether Media, Inc., Attention: Permissions Department, 6012 Blue Circle Drive, Minnetonka, MN 55343.

Library of Congress Cataloging-in-Publication Data

Names: Sabelko, Rebecca, author.
Title: Russia / by Rebecca Sabelko.
Description: Minneapolis, MN : Bellwether Media, 2023. | Series: Blastoff! Readers: Countries of the world | Includes bibliographical references and index. | Audience: Ages 5-8 | Audience: Grades 2-3 | Summary: "Relevant images match informative text in this introduction to Russia. Intended for students in kindergarten through third grade"– Provided by publisher.
Identifiers: LCCN 2022018176 (print) | LCCN 2022018177 (ebook) | ISBN 9781644877241 (library binding) | ISBN 9781648347702 (ebook)
Subjects: LCSH: Russia (Federation)–Juvenile literature.
Classification: LCC DK510.23 .S23 2023 (print) | LCC DK510.23 (ebook) | DDC 947–dc23/eng/20220414
LC record available at https://lccn.loc.gov/2022018176
LC ebook record available at https://lccn.loc.gov/2022018177

Text copyright © 2023 by Bellwether Media, Inc. BLASTOFF! READERS and associated logos are trademarks and/or registered trademarks of Bellwether Media, Inc.

Editor: Rachael Barnes   Designer: Gabriel Hilger

Printed in the United States of America, North Mankato, MN.

Table of Contents

All About Russia	4
Land and Animals	6
Life in Russia	12
Russia Facts	20
Glossary	22
To Learn More	23
Index	24

All About Russia

Moscow

Russia is the largest country in the world! It spreads across both Europe and Asia.

Russia is known for a kind of dance called **ballet**. The capital city is Moscow.

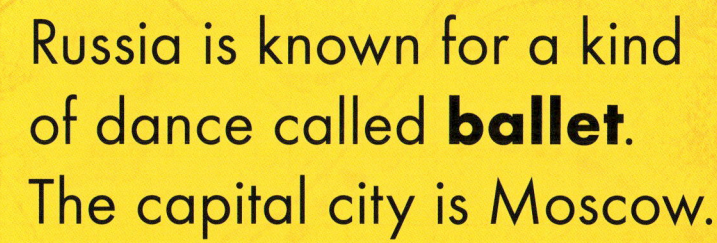

ballet dancers

Land and Animals

Tundra covers northern Russia. This area has short summers. Winters are long and cold.

Forests lie south of the tundra. This area is warmer. It gets little rain.

Plains cover western Russia. **Steppes** spread across the south.

The Ural Mountains rise between European and Asian Russia. The Lena River runs north through **Siberia**.

Ural Mountains

Lena River

Size: 2,734 miles (4,400 kilometers) long
Famous For: longest river entirely in Russia

Tigers sneak up on boars in Russia's forests. Cranes fly in the **wetlands**.

Siberian tiger

Brown bears **wander** the Ural Mountains. Seals swim in Lake Baikal.

Life in Russia

Most people in Russia are of Russian **heritage**. They speak Russian.

Tartars and other smaller groups live in the country. They speak their own languages.

Russians enjoy many sports. Soccer and hockey are favorites. *Lapta* is a lot like baseball.

People hike and garden. They travel to *dachas* in the country.

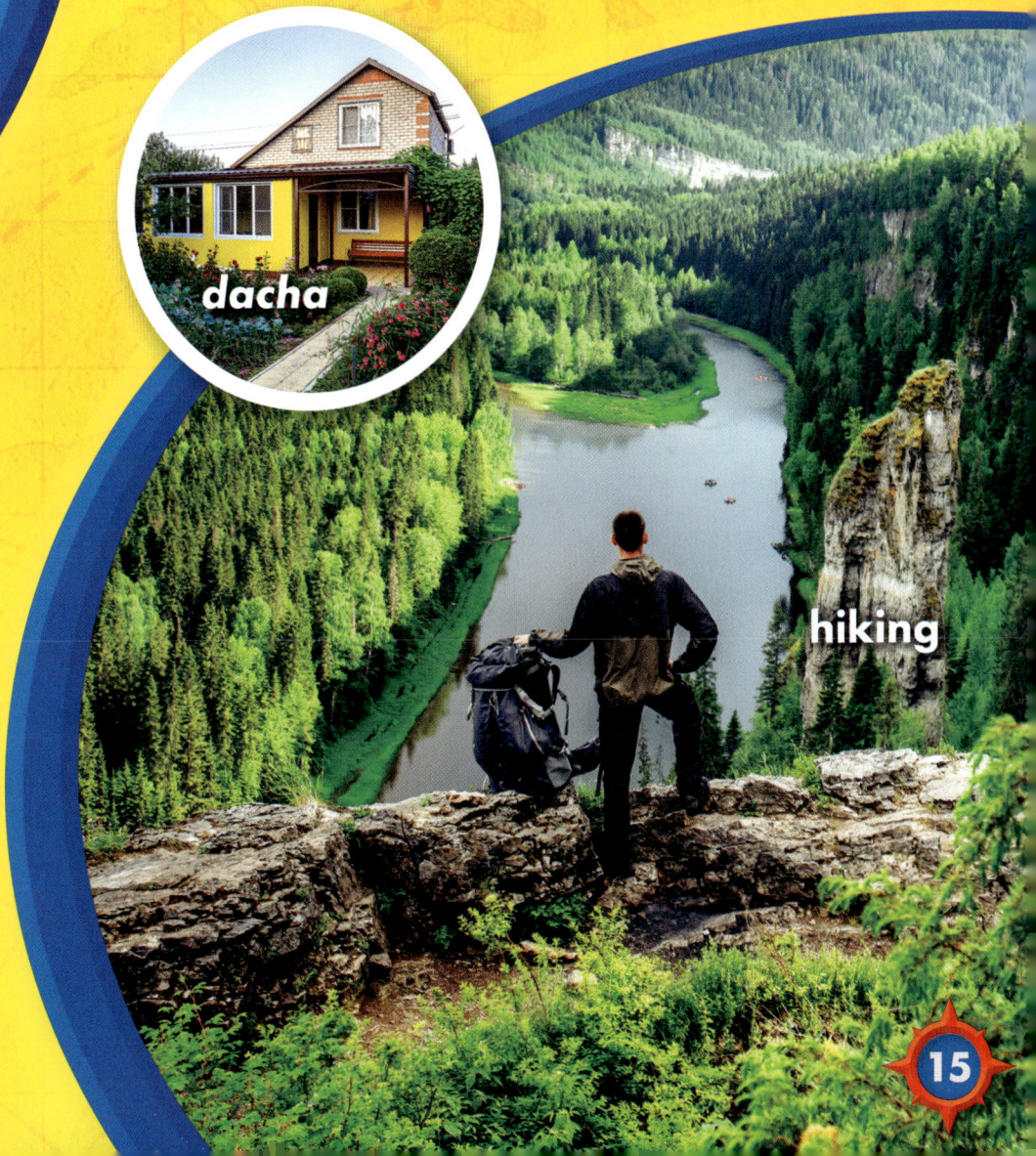

dacha

hiking

Kasha is a common hot breakfast food. *Pirozhki* are small buns stuffed with cabbage.

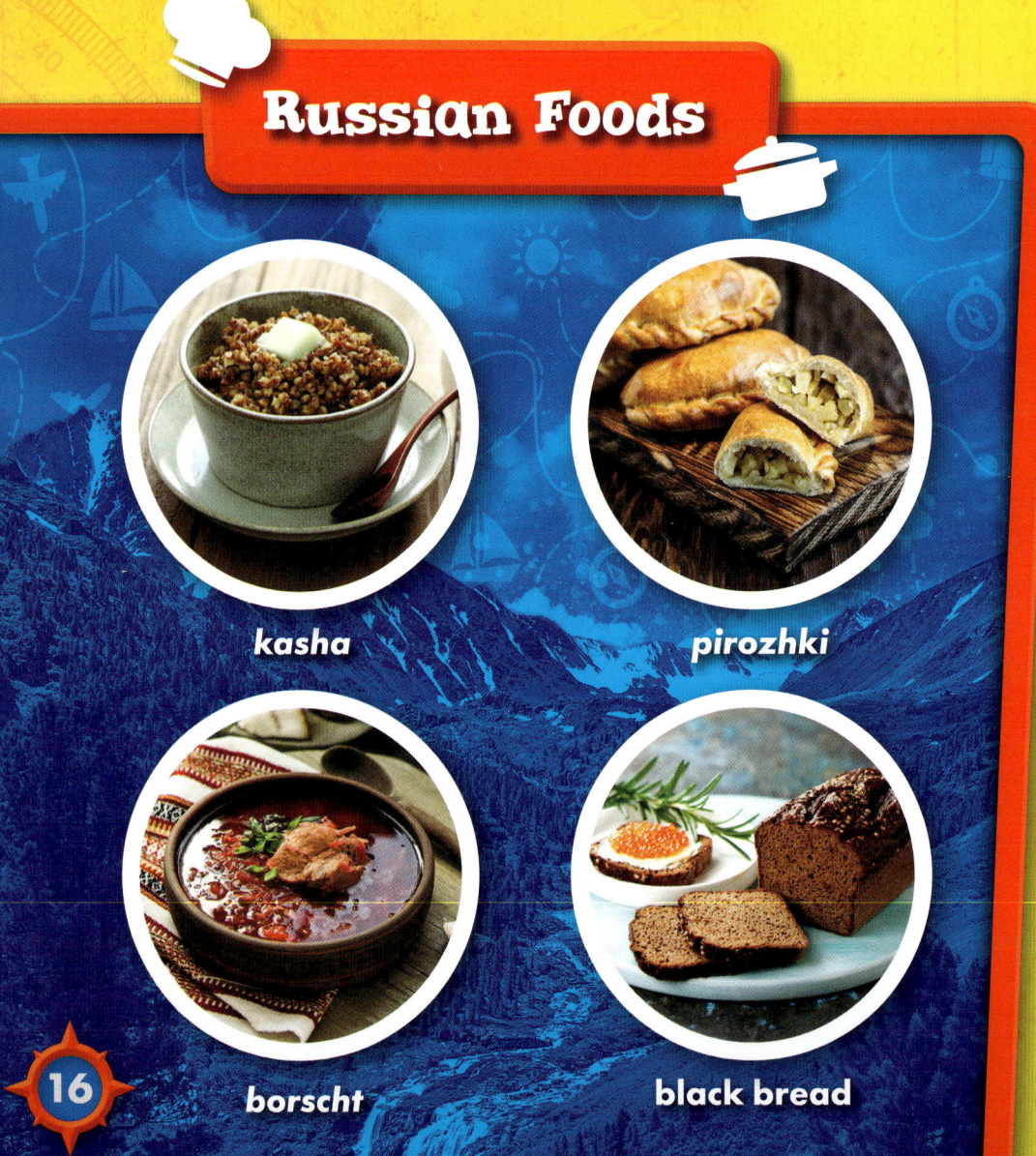

Russian Foods

kasha

pirozhki

borscht

black bread

Borscht is a **traditional** beet soup. Black bread is served at breakfast, lunch, and dinner.

The New Year is a favorite weeklong holiday.
Families decorate trees.
They eat special food.

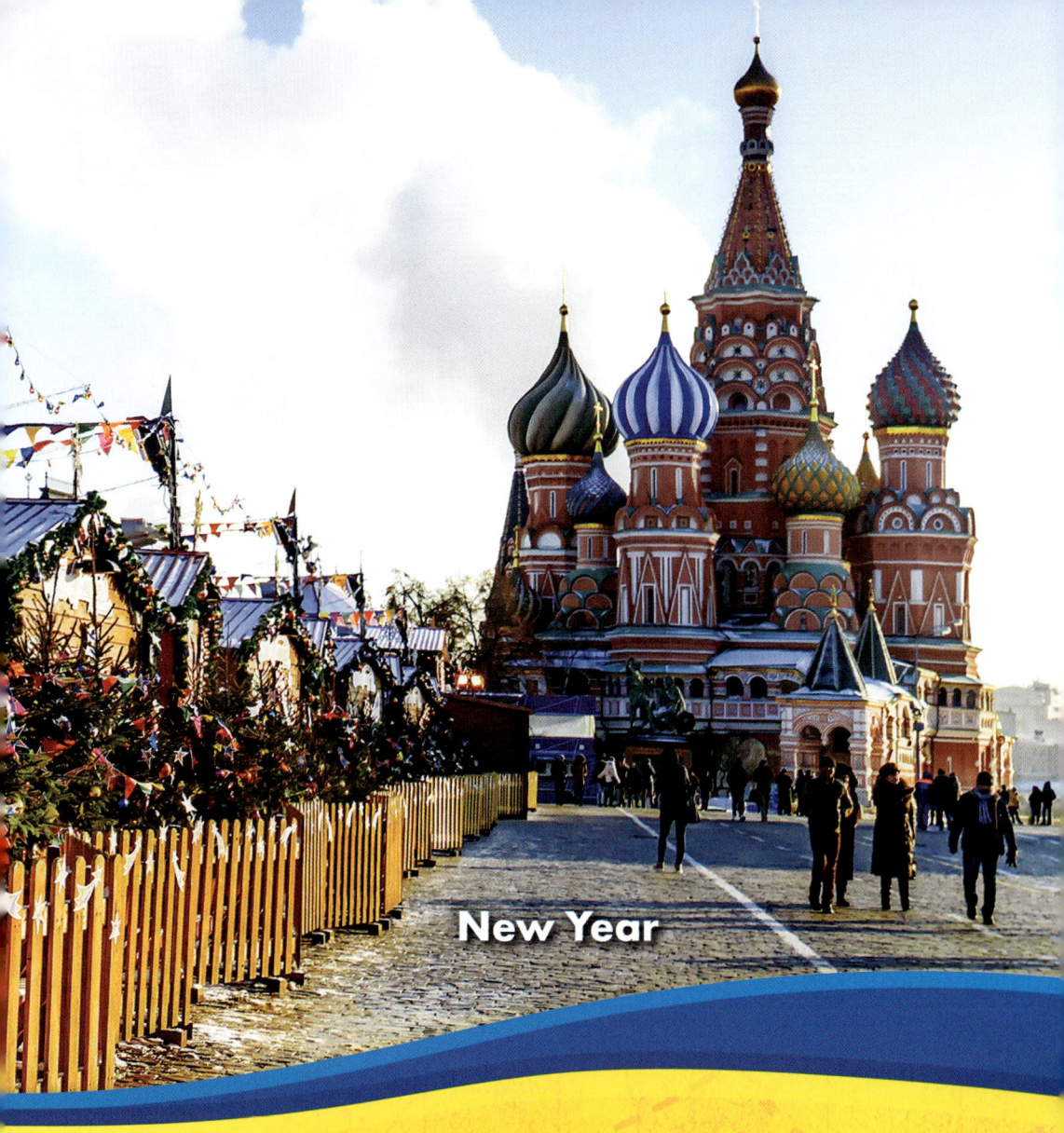

New Year

Russia Day is June 12. People honor their history and future!

Russia Facts

Size:
6,601,668 square miles
(17,098,242 square kilometers)

Population:
142,021,981 (2022)

National Holiday:
Russia Day (July 12)

Main Language:
Russian

Capital City:
Moscow

Famous Face

Name: Evgenia Medvedeva

Famous For: a figure skater who has won two Olympic silver medals and two world championships

Religions

- other or none: 63%
- other Christian: 2%
- Russian Orthodox: 20%
- Muslim: 15%

Top Landmarks

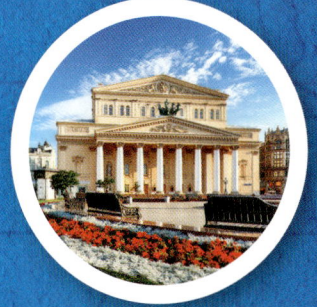
Bolshoi Theatre

Lake Baikal

Saint Basil's Cathedral

Glossary

ballet—a form of dance that tells a story

heritage—the backgrounds and beliefs that are part of the history of a group of people

plains—large areas of flat land

Siberia—a region in northern Asia that goes from the Ural Mountains to the Pacific Ocean; Siberia covers all of Asian Russia.

steppes—dry, flat land in areas with wide temperature ranges

traditional—related to customs, ideas, or beliefs handed down from one generation to the next

tundra—frozen, treeless land; beneath the surface, tundra is permafrost, or land that is permanently frozen.

wander—to move around without a specific direction

wetlands—areas of land that are covered with low levels of water for most of the year

To Learn More

AT THE LIBRARY

Dean, Jessica. *Russia*. Minneapolis, Minn.: Pogo, 2019.

Perdew, Laura. *Tour the Tundra: Biome Explorers*. Norwich, Vt.: Nomad Press, 2022.

Sherman, Jill. *Hockey*. Minneapolis, Minn.: Bellwether Media, 2020.

ON THE WEB

FACTSURFER

Factsurfer.com gives you a safe, fun way to find more information.

1. Go to www.factsurfer.com.

2. Enter "Russia" into the search box and click 🔍.

3. Select your book cover to see a list of related content.

Index

animals, 10, 11
Asia, 4, 8
ballet, 5
dachas, 15
Europe, 4, 8
families, 18
foods, 16, 17, 18
forests, 7, 10
garden, 15
hike, 15
hockey, 14
Lake Baikal, 11
languages, 12
lapta, 14
Lena River, 8, 9
map, 5
Moscow, 4, 5
New Year, 18, 19
people, 12, 15, 19
plains, 8
rain, 7
Russia Day, 19

Russia facts, 20–21
Russian (language), 12, 13
say hello, 13
Siberia, 8
size, 4
soccer, 14
steppes, 8
summers, 6
Tartars, 12
tundra, 6, 7
Ural Mountains, 8, 11
wetlands, 10
winters, 6

The images in this book are reproduced through the courtesy of: FOTOGRIN, front cover; straga, front cover; YURY TARANIK, pp. 2-3; pudiq, p. 3; Pavel Burchenko, pp. 4-5; df028, p. 5; Andrei Stepanov, pp. 6-7; AlxYago, p. 7; zorinjonny, p. 8; Vicky Ivanova, pp. 8-9; e X p o s e, pp. 10-11; Boris Dmitriev, p. 11 (wild boar); Ondrej Prosicky, p. 11 (common crane); Sergey Uryadnikov, p 11 (brown bear); Strelyuk, p. 11 (Baikal seal); TTstudio, pp. 12, 21 (Bolshoi Theatre); frantic00, pp. 12-13; Idea Studio, pp. 14-15; Alizada Studio, p. 14 (inset); Tatiana Zinchenko, p. 15 (inset); Sergei Cash, p. 15; bonchan, p. 16 (kasha); Isaeva Studio, p. 16 (pirozhki); Sokor Space, p. 16 (borscht); Y. A. Photo, p. 16 (black bread); p_ponomareva, p. 17; dimbar76, pp. 18-19; titoOnz, p. 20 (flag); Aflo Co. Ltd./ Alamy, p. 20 (Evgenia Medvedeva); Mikhail Markovskiy, p. 21 (Lake Baikal); Vjacheslav Lopatin, p. 21 (Saint Basil's Cathedral); GUDKOV ANDREY, pp. 22-23.